Enid Blyton
The Famous Five

FIVE HAVE A PUZZLING TIME

Cover illustration by Eileen Soper

The Famous Five – full-length adventures

1. Five On A Treasure Island
2. Five Go Adventuring Again
3. Five Run Away Together
4. Five Go to Smuggler's Top
5. Five Go Off in a Caravan
6. Five On Kirrin Island Again
7. Five Go Off to Camp
8. Five Get Into Trouble
9. Five Fall Into Adventure
10. Five on a Hike Together
11. Five Have a Wonderful Time
12. Five Go Down to the Sea
13. Five Go to Mystery Moor
14. Five Have Plenty of Fun
15. Five on a Secret Trail
16. Five Go to Billycock Hill
17. Five Get Into a Fix
18. Five on Finniston Farm
19. Five Go to Demon's Rocks
20. Five Have a Mystery to Solve
21. Five Are Together Again

Turn to the back of the book for more Famous Five,
and other books by Enid Blyton

Enid Blyton

The Famous Five

FIVE HAVE A PUZZLING TIME

Hodder
Children's
Books

a division of Hachette Children's Group

Five Have a Puzzling Time

IT WAS dark and very quiet in Kirrin Cottage – almost midnight. The Five were all in bed – yes, Timmy, the dog, too, for he was lying on George's feet, his usual place at night. He wasn't having a very comfortable time, because George, whose real name was Georgina, was so restless.

She tossed and turned and groaned – and at last awoke Anne, who was in the bed next to her.

'What's the matter, George?' said Anne, sleepily. 'Is your tooth aching again?'

'Yes, it's awful,' said George, sitting up with her hand to her cheek. 'Get off my feet, Timmy, I'll just *have* to get up and walk about!'

'Poor George,' said Anne. 'Good thing you're going to the dentist tomorrow!'

FIVE HAVE A PUZZLING TIME

'Don't remind me of that!' said George, walking up and down the bedroom. 'Go to sleep, Anne – I didn't mean to disturb you.'

The big clock in the hall downstairs struck twelve, very slowly and solemnly. Anne listened, then her eyes shut and she fell asleep again. George went to the window and looked out over Kirrin Bay, holding a hand to her painful cheek. Timmy jumped off the bed and stood beside her, paws on the windowsill. He knew that George was in pain, and he was troubled. He rested his head against her hand and gave it a tiny lick.

'Dear Timmy,' said George. 'I hope *you'll* never have toothache! You'd go mad! Look at Kirrin Bay – isn't it lovely? And you can just see Kirrin Island – *my* island, Timmy – looming up in the darkness!'

Suddenly George stiffened and frowned. She stared across the bay, and then turned and called urgently to Anne.

'Anne! Quick, wake up! ANNE! Come and see! There's a light shining out on Kirrin Island, a light,

I tell you! Somebody's there – on MY island! Anne, come and see!'

Anne sat up sleepily. 'What's the matter, George? What did you say?'

'I said there's a light on Kirrin Island! Somebody must be there – without permission too! I'll get my boat and row out right now!'

George was very angry indeed, and Timmy gave a little growl. He would most certainly deal with whoever it was on the island!

'Oh, George – don't be an idiot!' said Anne. 'As if you could get your boat and row across the bay in the middle of the night! You must be mistaken!' She jumped out of bed and went to the window. 'Where's this light?'

'It's gone – it went out just as you jumped out of bed,' said George. 'Who can be there, Anne? I'll wake the boys and tell them. We'll get my boat.'

She went quickly down to the room where Dick and Julian lay asleep and shook them roughly.

'Wake up! Oh, PLEASE wake up! Something's going on over at Kirrin Island. I saw a light there.

WAKE UP, Julian.'

George's excited voice not only woke up the boys, but her father as well. He sat up in bed in the next room, thinking there must be burglars in the house!

'Robbers, my dear!' he hissed in his wife's ear, making her start up in fright.

'Quentin, it's only the children!' said his wife, sleepily. 'I expect George's toothache is worse. I'll go and see.'

Everybody met in the boys' room. 'What on earth is all this about?' demanded George's father.

'There's a light on Kirrin Island,' said George, quite fiercely. 'On *my* island! I'm going to see who it is – and so is Timmy. If no one will come with me I'll go alone.'

'Indeed you won't go,' said her father, raising his voice angrily. 'Get back to bed! Rowing to Kirrin Island in the middle of the night! You must be mad. There *can't* be anyone there. You've had a bad dream, or something.'

'Dad, there's a *light* there – I saw it!' said George, in a voice as loud as her father's. He went at once to

4

the window and looked out. 'Rubbish!' he said. 'Not a glimmer of any sort to be seen! You dreamt it!'

'I did NOT!' said George, angrily. 'Somebody is there, I tell you. Trespassing!'

'Well, *let* them trespass!' said her father. 'You can go over tomorrow.'

'I *can't*!' almost wailed George. 'I've got to go to the dentist, and have this nasty, horrible, awful tooth out. I *must* go tonight!'

'Shut up, George,' said Julian. 'Be sensible. Whoever's there will still be there tomorrow. I'll go over with Dick. Anyway, there's no light there now – you probably made a mistake. Go to bed, for goodness' sake.'

George flung out of the boys' room, and went to her own, furious. Timmy went with her, licking her now and again. Why couldn't he and George go off together, this very minute? Timmy was quite ready to!

'Now my tooth's aching worse than ever!' said poor George, angry and miserable, dumping herself violently on her bed. Her mother came over to her with a glass of water and two small pills.

'Take these, George,' she said. 'Your tooth will soon stop aching. Please be sensible, dear.'

'That's one thing George can't be!' said Anne, 'Cheer up, George – that tooth will be gone tomorrow – and there won't be anyone on your island, you'll see – and everything will be right again'.

George grunted, and lay down with her aching cheek on her hand. She meant to slip out of bed, and go down to her boat as soon as the house was quiet again. But the little pills quickly did their work, and in five minutes her tooth had stopped aching, and she was fast asleep.

In the morning when she awoke, she remembered at once what she had seen the night before – a light on her island! And then she remembered the dentist – oh dear, two horrible thoughts – someone trespassing on her precious island – and a tooth to come out! She sat up in bed.

'Anne! My tooth has stopped aching. I won't go to the dentist, I'll go to Kirrin Island with

Timmy and the boys.'

But her father thought differently, and after a really furious battle between the hot-tempered George and her equally hot-tempered father, George was packed off with her mother in the car, for her visit to the dentist! Timmy went with her, quite alarmed at all the goings-on!

'Poor George,' said Anne, as the car went off down the road. 'She does get so worked up about things.'

'Well, anyone gets upset with toothache,' said Julian. He stared out over Kirrin Bay, which was as blue as cornflowers that morning. 'I wonder if George *did* see a light on the island last night? *You* didn't see one, did you, Anne, when you awoke?'

'No. It was all dark there,' said Anne. 'Honestly, I think George must have dreamt it! Anyway she can take out her boat this afternoon, and we'll go with her, and have a good look round – that should satisfy her!'

'She may not feel like doing anything except having a bit of a rest,' said Dick. 'She's had toothache for days now, and it does get you down. I tell you what – we three will get the boat and go over to the island this morning – then, when we find nothing and nobody there – except the rabbits and the jackdaws – we can tell George, and she won't worry any more!'

'Right!' said Julian. 'Let's go now, straight away! Uncle Quentin will be glad to be rid of us – he's working hard this morning on one of his newest problems.'

George's father was glad to hear that the three were going off for the morning.

'Now I'll have the house to myself,' he said, thankfully. 'Except for Joanna, of course. I hope she doesn't take it into her head to clean out the boiler this morning – I MUST have peace and quiet.'

'You ought to invent a boiler that cleans *itself* out with hardly a whisper!' said Anne, smiling at her uncle. 'Anyway, we'll be out of your way. We're just going!'

They went to the beach, to get George's boat. There it was ready and waiting! Julian looked across to where Kirrin Island lay peacefully in the sun. He was quite certain there was nobody there! George must have dreamt the light she had seen shining in the night.

'We'll row right round the island and see if there's a boat tied up anywhere, or beached,' said Dick, taking the oars. 'If there isn't, we'll know there's no one there. It's too far for anyone to swim to. Well – here we go!'

And away they went in the warm spring sunshine, the little waves lapping cheerfully round the boat.

Anne leaned back and let her hand dabble in the water – what fun to go over to the island and see all the rabbits – there would be young ones there too, now.

'Here we are, almost at the island,' said Julian. 'In and out of the rocks we go! I'm sorry for anyone who tries to come here in the middle of the night, unable to see what rocks to avoid! Not a sign of a boat anywhere – George *must* have dreamt it all!'

Dick rowed the boat carefully between the rocks that guarded the island.

'We'll land at our usual little cove,' he said. 'I bet

no one else would know how to get there if they didn't already know the way!'

A low wall of sharp rocks came into sight and Dick rounded it neatly. Now they could see the cove where they meant to land – a little natural harbour, with a calm inlet of water running up to a smooth stretch of sand.

'The water's like glass here,' said Anne. 'I can see the bottom of the cove.' She leapt out and helped the boys to pull in the boat.

'*Look* at the rabbits!' said Dick, as they walked up the smooth sandy beach. 'Tame as ever!'

A small baby rabbit came lolloping up to Anne. 'You sweet little thing!' she said, trying to pick it up. 'You're just like a toy bunny!' But the tiny creature lolloped away again.

'Good thing Timmy's not here,' said Julian. 'He always looks so miserable when he sees the rabbits, because he knows he mustn't chase them!'

They came to the old ruined castle that had been built long ago on the island. The ancient, broken-down entrance led into a great yard, overgrown with weeds. Now the jackdaws came down from the tower, and chacked loudly round them in a very friendly manner. Some of them flew down to the children's feet, and walked about as tame as hens in a farmyard.

'Well – it doesn't look as if anyone's here,' said Julian, staring round and about.

'And there was no boat anywhere,' said Anne. 'So how could anyone have come here? Let's see if there are any signs of a fire having been lit. The flames would be seen at night, if so.'

They began to hunt all around. They went in and out of the old castle, examining the floor – but there was no sign of anyone having made a fire.

'If George saw a light, then there must be a lamp or lantern somewhere,' said Dick. 'Anne, did she see the light high up on the island – as if it came from the tower?'

'She didn't say,' said Anne. 'But I should *think* it must have been high up. We'll go up the old broken-down tower steps as far as we can, shall we? We might see something there – perhaps a lantern. It's possible, I suppose, that someone might have been signalling for some reason!'

But, no matter how they searched, the three could find nothing to explain the light that George had said she saw.

'Let's go and lie down on the grass, and watch the rabbits,' said Anne. 'Hey – why did the jackdaws all fly up then – and why are they chacking so much? What frightened them?'

'Funny!' said Julian, staring at the big black birds, circling round and round above them, calling 'chack-chack-chack' so excitedly. '*We* didn't scare them, I'm sure. I suppose there *can't* be someone else here?'

'Well – we'll walk round the island and examine the rocks sticking up here and there,' said Dick, puzzled about the jackdaws, too. 'Someone might be hiding behind one of them.'

'I'm going to take off my sandals,' said Anne. 'I love running on the smooth sand in bare feet. I'll have a paddle, too – the water's quite warm today!'

The boys wandered off round the island. Anne sat

down and undid her sandals. She set them by a big stone, so that she could easily find them again, and ran down to the sea. Little waves were splashing over the smooth golden sand, and Anne ran into them, curling up her toes in pleasure.

'It's really almost warm enough to swim,' she thought. 'What a lovely little island this is – and how lucky George is to own it. I wish *I* had an island belonging to my family, that I could call my own. If I had, I suppose I'd worry, too, like George, if I thought anyone was trespassing here – scaring the rabbits – and even perhaps snaring them!'

Soon Julian and Dick came back together, having gone all round the island, and looked into every cranny. They called to Anne.

'Hello, paddler! Is the water nice and warm? We should have brought our swimming things.'

'We haven't seen a sign of a single soul,' said Dick. 'Better go home again. George may be back by now – wanting to tell us about her tooth, and what she's been through. Poor George!'

'I'll put on my sandals,' said Anne, drying her feet

by scrabbling them in the warm sand. She ran to the big stone by which she had put them. She stopped – and stared in surprise.

'What's happened to one of my sandals? Dick – Ju – have you taken one? Where have you put it?'

'Sandals? No – we didn't even know where you'd put them,' said Julian. 'There's one of them there, look – the other must be somewhere near.'

But it wasn't. No matter how they all looked, only one of Anne's sandals could be found!

'*Well*! How silly!' said Anne, amazed. 'I *know* I put them both together, just here. I know I did! Anyway, there's no one to take one of my sandals – and even if there were, why take one, and not both?'

'Perhaps a rabbit took one?' suggested Dick, with a grin. 'Or a jackdaw – they're really mischievous birds, you know!'

'A jackdaw surely couldn't pick up a *sandal*!' said Anne. 'It'd be too heavy. And I can't *imagine* a rabbit running off with one!'

'Well – it's not there,' said Dick, thinking to himself that Anne must have been mistaken about putting them both by the big stone. He hunted round, but could not see the other one anywhere – strange! However – there certainly was no one on the island – and, if there had been, someone wouldn't have been so silly as to risk being discovered by stealing one little sandal, in full view of Anne!

'We'll have to leave your sandal, wherever it is, Anne,' said Julian, at last. 'We ought to get back. Well – the only thing we can tell George is that we saw no one at all here – but that one sandal mysteriously disappeared!'

'Oh no!' said Anne, not bothering to put on her one sandal. 'Now I'll have to spend some of my precious pocket money to buy a pair of new sandals. How annoying!'

'Come on,' said Dick, going down towards their boat. 'George'll have a fit if we don't turn up soon. She'll think that the owner of the mysterious light has caught us and made us prisoners! Hurry up, Anne.'

They were soon all in the boat again, and the boys took it in turn to row back. Through the crowd of rocks they went, threading their way carefully, and at last came to their own beach.

George was there, waiting for them, Timmy beside her!

'You went without me!' she scolded. 'You really are horrible! What did you find?'

'Nothing and no one. The island's absolutely empty except for its usual inhabitants – rabbits and jackdaws!' said Julian, dragging the boat up the sand. 'Your strange light in the night must have been a dream, George!'

'It was NOT!' said George, and her voice was so angry that Timmy began to bark. 'You don't know where to look! Now if Timmy had been with you, he'd have smelt out anyone there – he'd have found the lamp or lantern – he'd have . . .'

'All right, all right – but we didn't *have* Timmy!' said Dick.

'How's the tooth, George?' said Anne, seeing that George's cheek was still swollen. 'Did you have it out? Did it hurt?'

But George didn't want to waste time in talking

about her tooth. 'It's out,' she said, shortly. 'Horrible tooth! If I hadn't had to go to the dentist, I could have gone with you – and I BET Timmy and I would have found something. I just BET we would!'

'All right – go there, then – and take Tim with you,' said Dick, exasperated.

'That's just what I *will* do!' said George with a scowl. '*We'll* soon find out who's hiding there. I'll go this afternoon – with Timmy. You can come, too, if you like, of course – but I can't see that you'll be much use!'

'Oh, we'll come all right!' said Dick. 'Even if it's only to say, "Told you so" when you can't find more than we did!'

George had made up her mind to go off in her boat after she had had her dinner.

'Although my mouth is so sore I'm sure I won't be able to eat anything!' she said. However, she ate as much as any of the others! Timmy sat very close to her, sad that she was cross and upset.

It wasn't a very happy meal. Uncle Quentin was

quiet and moody, for his work hadn't gone well that morning. Aunt Fanny looked worried.

George sulked. Timmy kept giving heavy sighs. Even Joanna the cook added a few cross words as she cleared away the dinner.

'I'd like to know who's been at the grapes and the oranges,' she said. '*Someone* came downstairs in the night and helped themselves. And George – what did you do with the bag of dog biscuits that came from the grocer's yesterday? I couldn't find any for Tim's dinner.'

'Oh don't fuss, Joanna!' said George. 'You know where I always put them – in the outhouse, with the chicken food.'

'Well, you didn't this time,' said Joanna, huffily.

'You can't have *looked*,' said George. 'Oh dear – why do all these things have to happen when I've a bad tooth?'

'Well – you certainly *shouldn't* have a bad tooth now,' remarked Julian. 'I thought the dentist . . .'

'All right, all right – yes, he *did* pull it out, but it still feels as if it's there,' said George, crossly.

'You'd better have a lie down this afternoon, George,' said her mother. 'A little sleep will . . .'

'Put you right!' chorused Julian, Dick and Anne, who had heard this saying of their aunt's a hundred times.

She laughed. 'Well – what with toothache all night, and little sleep, it's no wonder poor George is cross.'

'I'm NOT cross!' roared George, furiously, and that made everyone laugh, of course. Julian gave her a pat on the back.

'Cheer up. We'll all go and hunt over the island again this afternoon – and I expect you'll find a couple of pirates, two or three robbers, a shipwrecked sailor, a . . .'

George gave a sudden grin. 'Shut up, you idiot. Don't take any notice of me for a bit. I'll be all right soon.'

And she was. She took herself in hand, helped Joanna with the washing up, and then went to look for the biscuits for Timmy. Sure enough, they were missing, as Joanna had said.

'I'm *sure* I put them in the outhouse here,' said George, looking all around. 'I suppose I couldn't have. What *have* I done with them? Poor Tim – you'll have to make do with scraps, I'm afraid, till the butcher boy comes with your meat this afternoon. And by the way, Joanna, I did NOT come down last night and take grapes and oranges. My tooth was much too bad. And *I'd* like to know something now. Who's been at my big box of chocolates?'

She had opened a large box, and was staring inside. 'There's more than half gone!' she said. 'Timmy – have you been at them? Were you so hungry, poor thing?'

'Well, I must say that if he took them he was clever to put back the lid!' said Joanna. 'Maybe you ate an orange or two as well, Timmy-dog?'

'Woof,' said Timmy, in disgust, and turned his back on Joanna. As if he would steal chocolates or oranges!

George went off to find her mother. 'Mum – I feel better now. The swelling in my mouth is going down at top speed. I'll be all right to take the boat out with the others, really I will.'

'Well – your dad does want peace and quiet this afternoon,' said her mother. 'Go along, then – and don't get over-tired – you had quite a bad time this morning.'

Within ten minutes all the Five were in the boat once more. George was her old self again, and Julian grinned at her.

'Well? All set to find what we couldn't find? I must admit that with Timmy to help us, we're much more likely to be successful!'

They soon came to the island. George circled it deftly in the boat, being anxious herself to see that no one had hidden a boat anywhere. She pointed to where a great mass of brown seaweed had piled up on the west shore.

'See what the wind did when we had that terrific gale on Tuesday – brought in masses of seaweed again! Now we'll have an awful smell when it dries out! Hey – what's wrong with the jackdaws, all of a sudden? They're never scared of *us*! Why are they flying up in such a hurry? There *is* someone on the island!'

That's what *we* thought this morning,' said Dick, with a grin. 'But there wasn't! Plenty of rabbits, though – hundreds. Thank goodness there's *one* place left where they can live in peace!'

George swung the boat round and ran it deftly into the little cove. Out they all leapt, and pulled in the boat. Timmy jumped out first and tore up the beach at full speed, barking.

'That'll scare the life out of anyone hiding!' said George, pleased. 'Go on, Tim – bark. Hunt around! Sniff everywhere!'

The rabbits scattered at once when they heard Timmy. 'Don't you dare to touch them!' George called to him, knowing how much he longed to catch one. 'Heel, now, Timmy, heel! I want you to come round every corner of the island with me.'

Timmy ran to heel, his long tail swinging happily. He loved Kirrin Island. George set off, meaning to examine every well-loved corner, every possible hiding place. They came to a group of bushes and Timmy began to sniff about at once.

'He can smell something there!' said George, excited. 'What is it, Tim?'

But apparently he found nothing of interest, and soon joined them again. Then Anne's sharp eyes caught sight of something bright under a bush and she bent down to see what it was. She looked round at the others, astonished.

'Look – orange peel! Someone *must* have been here then! We'd never leave orange peel about! And look, what's *this*!'

They all clustered round and looked where Anne was pointing. George bent down and picked up something very small.

'See – a pip – a pip from a grape. Does that ring a bell, anyone?'

'Yes!' said Dick. 'Joanna said we'd been at the oranges and grapes – do you think that . . .'

'No! Who's going to steal a bit of fruit and take it over to the island to eat!' said Julian. 'That's too far-fetched, honestly! Let's be sensible!'

'What's Timmy doing?' said Anne, suddenly.

'Hey, Tim – don't scrape all the sand off the island!'

Timmy was feverishly scraping at the sand nearby with his front paws. He gave an excited little bark, that sounded pleased. What on earth had he found? The others ran to him at once.

Timmy had made a hole – and in it something showed – it seemed like a bulky bag of some kind. Timmy took hold of it with his teeth, and pulled. It split at once – and to everyone's enormous astonishment, out came a mass of dog biscuits!

How they stared! DOG biscuits! Surely, surely they couldn't be the biscuits that George had bought for Timmy the day before, and put in the outhouse?

'They *are*!' said George. 'Look – exactly the same kind. Isn't this strange! Who on earth would want to steal dog biscuits and bring them here – and oranges and grapes – and for goodness' sake, WHY?'

Nobody could think of an answer. Timmy began to crunch up the biscuits, looking very pleased indeed with himself. He didn't know who had buried them on Kirrin Island, but he thought it was a very good idea!

'Well, that settles it,' said Julian. 'You were right, George – someone is here – and you *did* see a light on the island in the middle of the night. But how did they get here without a boat?'

'We'll soon find out!' said George grimly. 'We know he's a thief, anyway! Tim – go to it! Find him, find him, whoever he is! Smell him out, Tim, smell him out!'

And off went Tim at once, nose to the ground, following the scent of the thief – now WHERE would he lead them? And whoever would he find? It really was too exciting for words.

Timmy went off at such a speed that the four couldn't keep up with him. He raced off round the castle, nose to ground, barking loudly.

'He'll certainly warn anyone in hiding that he's on their track,' panted Dick. 'Where on earth can they be? We've hunted everywhere!'

Over the sand and on to the rocks went Timmy, right up to where the seaweed was piled in great masses by the wind and the waves. He stopped and began to sniff anxiously.

'He's lost the trail!' said George, disappointed. 'It's the smell of the seaweed that's put him off.'

'Or else whoever was here came in a boat at high tide, which would bring it to the shore – and has sailed off again now the tide has gone out,' said Julian, frowning. 'There wouldn't be any trail to smell, then. Honestly, there doesn't seem to be *anyone* hiding – and now that even Tim is stumped, I think we're too late to find whoever it was.'

'Timmy – sniff round again,' said George. 'Go on – you may pick up some other trail.'

Timmy obediently sniffed here and there, and occasionally gave a strange growl of anger. Why? George was puzzled.

'Why does he sound so fierce?' she said. 'Really angry! What is it, Timmy?'

'Perhaps he doesn't like the smell of whoever has been here,' said Anne. 'Let's sit down for a bit and watch the rabbits and the jackdaws. Ju, did you bring any biscuits? I brought some barley sugars, and Dick's brought some chocolate in his pocket – I hope it won't be melted!'

George wanted to go on hunting, but the others felt that it was no use. If Timmy had found the scent, and couldn't follow it, no one else would be able to! Anyway, probably the trespasser was far away by now, safely in his boat!

Anne chose a sunny corner by an old ruined wall, and they sat down. At first the rabbits kept away from the children and Timmy – but soon they came out again, as tame as ever. The jackdaws came down too, running almost up to the children, hoping for a titbit.

Suddenly one jackdaw ran at a baby rabbit and gave it a hard peck in the back of the neck. The tiny thing fell over dazed, and all the jackdaws came round it in excitement.

'Oh, they'll *all* peck it now!' cried Anne, jumping up. 'Shoo, you birds!'

The birds flew off, chacking loudly, and the little rabbit began to crawl away, still dazed. It tried to run when the children went after it to pick it up, and disappeared under a bush.

'We'll have to get it out to make sure it's not *really*

hurt,' said Anne, anxiously. So the boys crawled under the bush, trying to find where the tiny creature had hidden itself. As it was a gorse bush it was very prickly, and Dick groaned.

'I'm being torn to pieces by these thorns. The rabbit's gone, Anne. I think it's found a rabbit hole and gone down it. I expect its mother's down there. She'll lick it better.'

They went back to where they had left their biscuits and bars of chocolate. Anne stopped suddenly and stared down in amazement.

'Look! Half the biscuits have gone – and two of the chocolate bars! Surely the jackdaws couldn't have taken them so quickly!'

'There's a broken biscuit over here, look – it must have been dropped by whoever stole them!' said Dick, amazed. 'What a nerve to come right up to where we were sitting, and take the things just when our backs were turned. I didn't hear a thing!'

'Nor did Tim – or he would have barked,' said George, really puzzled. 'Whoever it was must have come up as quietly as a mouse!'

'Let Timmy sniff round – he'll pick up the trail,' said Julian. 'It'll be so fresh!' Timmy was already sniffing, looking very puzzled indeed. The trail didn't seem much use to him! He ran a little way, nose to ground, following it – and then stopped, as if the trail had come to an end!

'Look, Timmy – trails don't finish all of a sudden!' said George, exasperated. 'People don't take off in mid-air!'

'There's a tree nearby,' said Anne. 'Do you think whoever it was could have climbed up into it?'

'Anne, there's NOBODY up the tree,' said George, in a patient, what-an-idiot-you-are sort of voice. 'I've looked.'

'Well, let's hunt round a bit again,' said Julian, more puzzled than ever. 'I know – we'll leave some biscuits and the bag of barley sugars here, and go behind that big gorse bush and hide – and maybe the thief, whoever he is, will come along and take *those*. He seems to have a sweet tooth!'

'Good idea,' said Dick. 'Come on, everyone – you too, Timmy – and not a sound from anyone, mind!'

They went behind the gorse bush and waited. Dick peeped out once or twice, but the bag of barley sugars remained untouched. Then suddenly Timmy gave a low growl, leapt out from behind the gorse bush and ran at something! Everyone followed in excitement. Who was it?

There was nobody there! But up on one of the branches of the nearby tree sat the thief, a barley sugar clutched in his hand, chattering angrily.

'It's a monkey – a little *monkey*!' cried George, in the greatest astonishment. 'It was *he* who took the other things! Wherever did he come from?'

The monkey leapt to the top of a broken wall, chattered again at them, and disappeared. Timmy raced to the wall, but the monkey was nowhere to be seen.

'Well – what do you think of *that*?' said Dick. 'A monkey! Where has he come from? Somebody must have brought him here – but why? And is that somebody still here – or has he gone?'

'I bet it was that monkey who came and stole my sandal this morning!' said Anne, suddenly.

'Of course!' said Julian. 'This *is* a puzzle! What do we do next?'

'Well, there's one thing we *do* know – and that is that a monkey wouldn't light a fire or a lamp at night on the island,' said Dick. 'That must have been done by a human being – and he MUST still be on the island if his monkey's here. He surely wouldn't go away and leave the little thing to starve.'

'Oh, *no* – it's such a sweet little creature,' said Anne. 'It had a really comical little face – did you notice? Thank goodness it left us most of the barley sugars. Let's have some, before anything else happens!'

They sat sucking the barley sugars, really puzzled. 'Buried dog biscuits!' said Julian. 'A monkey that steals food – and sandals! By the way, let's go and have a look at where we left those dog biscuits – maybe they've gone as well!'

They went off to see – but no, there were the scattered biscuits. Timmy helped himself to a few again, and a loud crunching filled the air. The jackdaws hopped near, hoping to pick up a few crumbs. Timmy ran at them, and then stopped and put his nose down to the ground. He had picked up the same scent as before!

'Follow the trail again, Tim,' said Julian. 'You may do better this time. Go on!'

But before Timmy could even put his head down again to follow it, something odd happened. A strange noise came from the west side of the island – the miserable howling of a dog!

'That's a *dog*!' cried Dick, amazed. 'On the island, too – whatever next! Where is he?'

'Oh, quick – he sounds as if he's in trouble!' cried George. 'What's happening? Quick, Julian, quick, Timmy! Oh, poor thing, there he goes, howling again. We must find him, we must!'

The Five set off in the direction of the howls, Timmy racing ahead anxiously. He knew far better than the others that a dog was in sore trouble – a howling of that kind meant not only pain, but terror. But how did a dog come to be on the island – and a monkey, too! Timmy was as puzzled as the children.

Julian was now in front of the other three, and was heading for the seaweed-spread shore on the west of the island. George suddenly gave a cry, and pointed.

'There's the monkey again! He's seen us – he's racing away!'

'Maybe he'll lead us to wherever the dog is,' shouted Julian. The monkey scampered in front, just ahead of Timmy. They all came to the shore, and stopped when they came to the piled-up heaps of brown, slippery seaweed, covering the rocks in great masses.

'The dog's stopped howling,' said George, looking all round. 'I'm sure he must be somewhere near here. What's the monkey doing? Look – he's running out over the seaweed. He'll slip into a pool and drown!'

They watched the tiny brown monkey. He was making his way over the seaweed-covered rocks now, avoiding the pools of water here and there. Further and further out he went. George started to go, too, but Julian pulled her back.

'No. That seaweed is slippery – it's too dangerous to go out on those rocks – we know the sea is very deep in between. *Look* at that little monkey – where on earth does he think he's going?'

The monkey came to a rock that was absolutely covered with thick masses of seaweed flung there by the surging, wind-blown tide. He had no sooner arrived there than an extraordinary thing happened!

A small mass of seaweed moved – and out of it came something that made the Five stare in utter disbelief.

'It can't be!' muttered Dick. 'No – it *can't* be!'

It was the brown and white head of a big dog!

The Five stared, unable to move. Never had they expected to see such a thing! The head suddenly opened a great mouth and howled dismally! In a flash, Timmy was over the seaweed-y rocks, barking for all he was worth as if to say, 'Hold on, friend, I'm coming!'

And then another surprising thing happened! A second head poked up from under a covering of seaweed, and a voice shouted loudly, 'Tell your dog to keep off! Mine will fight him! And go away, all of you!'

The Five were so full of amazement that they stood like statues, unable to say a word. Then George, afraid that the hidden dog might attack Timmy, yelled to him.

'Tim! Come back! Tim, do you hear me? Heel, Tim, heel!'

Timmy turned, and came back very sulkily, his tail down. *Why* had George called him back at such an exciting moment? He had only wanted to help the other dog!

The second head was still poking out of its strange seaweed-y hiding place – the head of a small boy! Julian really could not believe his eyes. So *that* was the hiding place – under the seaweed – and the dog was there, too – and probably the monkey had hidden there as well! What *was* going on?

'Hey, you there in the seaweed – come on out!' yelled Julian. 'We won't hurt you. If you want help, we'll give it to you. Come on out, and tell us what you're doing!'

'All right. But if you try to catch me, I'll set my dog on you!' yelled back a defiant voice. 'He's a cross-bred Alsatian and he could eat up your dog in one gulp!'

'We won't do anything to hurt you or your dog,' yelled back Dick. 'We heard him howling, poor thing. He's terrified of being under the seaweed. COME ON OUT!'

And then the seaweed pile was heaved up and down, and out came a scraggy, wet boy of about eleven. He pulled the seaweed off the dog, who was quite weighted down by it. The great animal shook itself, and gave one more miserable howl.

'You look out for your dog!' yelled the boy. 'Mine's fierce. There'll be a terrible fight if yours goes for mine.'

But Timmy had no idea of fighting such a wet, miserable and hungry dog! He waited until the boy and the Alsatian came scrambling towards the Five, over the rocks, and then he leapt lightly over the seaweed, and ran to the great Alsatian, his long tail wagging in welcome. He whined a little to him, and then licked his face, as if to say, 'Cheer up! I'm your friend!'

The Alsatian gave a little growl – and then an apologetic bark. He wagged his wet tail, and then, side by side with Timmy, ran up the shore to the waiting children.

The boy came scrambling along next, the little monkey now chattering on his shoulder, holding on to the boy's hair to save himself from falling.

The Five were almost too astonished to say a word, but the two dogs made up for their silence by racing along the beach, barking madly. The boy looked half scared, half sulky, and stared at them defiantly. George spoke to him first.

'What are you doing on my island?'

'Nothing,' said the boy. 'I just came here – with my dog and monkey – for – well – for a little holiday.'

'How did you come here?' asked Julian. 'We didn't see any boat.'

'I didn't *come* in a boat,' said the boy. 'Well, what *did* you come in, then?' asked Dick, astonished. 'I won't tell you,' said the boy. 'If I did you'd take it away from me – and, and . . .'

And then, to the dismay of the Five he began to cry bitterly, tears pouring down his cheeks. The little monkey put his arms round the boy's neck and loved him, and the dog leapt up, licking him wherever he could, whining in sympathy.

'Oh, don't cry like that!' said Anne, horrified. She took the boy's hand and led him along the beach. 'It's all right. We're your friends. We like your monkey and your dog. Tell us what's the matter. We'll help you!'

Soon they were all sitting down, the monkey still on the boy's shoulder, the dog close beside him. Even Timmy sat as close to the boy as he could, upset because of his tears.

'Have a barley sugar?' said Dick. 'Take two. That's right. Now, tell us what's been happening? Why did you come here – and how?'

'There's not much to tell,' said the boy. 'My name's Bobby Loman. I live with my Granpop in Kirrin Village. My mum and dad are dead, and I'm on my own – except for Chippy the monkey here, and Chummy, my Alsatian. I've run away. That's all.'

'No,' said Anne gently. 'That isn't all. Tell us *everything*, Bobby.'

'Oh, well – it's not much,' said Bobby. 'Granpop hates Chippy, my monkey, because he steals things. And Chummy costs a lot to keep – and – and – you see, he bit someone last week – and Granpop said he was to be put to sleep. Chummy, killed. He's my best friend! There's nobody he loves better than me, you don't know how kind and good he is, he sleeps on my bed at night, he licks me when things are bad, he – he . . .'

Bobby began to cry again, and the Alsatian nestled close to him and licked his cheek. 'See what I mean?' said Bobby. 'He loves me! He's the only person who does – and I WON'T have him put to sleep. Well – would you have this nice dog of *yours* killed?'

'NO! Never, never, NEVER!' said George, and put her arms round a surprised Timmy. 'You're quite right to run away, Bobby. I'm GLAD you came to my island. VERY glad. You and Chippy and Chummy can live here as long as you like. We'll bring you food each day, we'll . . .'

'Hold on, George,' said Julian. 'Don't make promises we can't keep. Let's go back to Kirrin Cottage and tell your mum about this – she'll know what's best to do. Bobby can stay with us, perhaps, till things are settled.'

'Oh – what fun to have another dog *and* a monkey, as well as Timmy,' said Anne. 'Bobby – how did you come to the island, if you didn't have a boat?'

'Oh – that was easy,' said Bobby. 'I've got one of those blow up beds. Chippy and I sailed on it, with a spade for an oar – and Chummy swam alongside. It's buried in the sand, so that nobody would see it. But I didn't have any food, so . . .'

'So you crept into our outhouse last night and took a bag of dog biscuits for Chummy, and some fruit for Chippy,' said Julian. 'What about yourself?'

'Oh – I've been eating the dog biscuits,' said Bobby. 'I took some chocolates too, and ate those. I'm sorry about the stealing. I was sort of – sort of – desperate, you know. I'll pay back for everything I took.'

'Come on – let's get back home,' said Julian,

seeing that Bobby was tired out, cold, wet, and probably very hungry. Come along now – we'll get our boat!'

The Five went back to where they had left George's boat, and took Bobby, Chippy, the monkey and Chummy the Alsatian with them. Timmy was very kind to them all, and wagged his tail hard the whole time, to show how friendly he was.

'I'm a bit scared of seeing your mum and dad,' said Bobby, in the boat. 'You're sure they won't send me off to a children's home – or to prison, or something like that? Chummy here would fret like anything if I went away from him.'

'I don't think you need worry,' said Julian, who was rowing. 'And I wouldn't be surprised if your Granpop was very pleased to hear you're safe.'

Bobby looked doubtful, but said no more. He cuddled up to Timmy and Chummy, who both took turns at licking him. Chippy the monkey was very lively and leapt from one person to another, making a funny little chattering noise. He took Dick's handkerchief out of his pocket and pretended to blow his nose on it.

'Hey – you're not to take things from people, I've told you that before!' said Bobby. 'Ooooh – that reminds me – he brought this shoe to me this morning – does it belong to any of you?'

And out of his pocket he took – one red sandal!

Anne gave a delighted yell. 'OH! It's mine. I missed it this morning. Oh *good* – now I won't have to buy a new pair! Chippy – you really are a monkey!'

'There's no doubt about *that*!' said Dick grinning, and Chippy made his chattering noise as if he understood every word!

George's mother was very astonished to see a monkey, a dog and another boy added to the Five when they arrived at Kirrin Cottage.

'Who are all these?' she said. 'I don't mind the dog, George, but I will *not* have a monkey running loose in the house.'

'He can sleep in the shed, Mum,' said George. 'Please don't say he can't. Mum, this is Bobby – he ran away from his grandfather who wanted to put his lovely dog to sleep.'

'Bobby? Bobby Loman do you mean?' said Mrs Kirrin at once. 'He was in the papers today – and a picture of the dog and the monkey too! Bobby, your grandfather is very unhappy and worried. You were a silly little boy to run away just because of an upset. I'm sure your grandfather would never have had your dog destroyed. He only said that in the heat of the moment – when he was very cross!'

Bobby looked rather scared at Mrs Kirrin's forthright words. George put her arm around his shoulder.

'Mum!' she said, 'I'm sure *I'd* run away if you threatened to do anything to Timmy – so I do understand why Bobby ran away to my island. Well – *sailed* away!'

'Oh – so *that's* who it was on your island last night!' said Mrs Kirrin. 'Well, well, well! You Five do seem to run into adventure, don't you? How did he get there? And what was the light you saw?'

'I floated there on my air bed,' said Bobby. 'Oh – I've forgotten it! It's still on the island. The light George saw was my torch, I expect. I was

43

looking for somewhere safe to sleep. I never imagined anyone would see the light of a torch in the dark of midnight!'

'Oh, you don't know George!' said Dick. 'If anyone happened to strike even a match on her beloved island, she'd be sure to be looking out of the window at that very moment, and see the flare. Then we'd all have to go rushing off to find out what it was.'

'Shut up,' said George, crossly. 'It's a good thing I did look out of the window last night – if I hadn't, goodness knows what would have happened to Bobby and the monkey and Chummy – they might have starved to death.'

'Well, we still had plenty of dog biscuits left,' said Bobby. 'They weren't bad – but very hard. I got Chummy to bite them in half for me.'

'How very disgusting!' said Mrs Kirrin. 'Now let's think what's best to do. What's your grandfather's phone number, Bobby? I'll ring him up at once, and then you can go home. I hope you'll tell him you're sorry for being such a silly boy!'

'Er, Mum – I've asked Bobby to stay the night,' said George. 'Mum, the monkey's so sweet. You'll love him. And Chummy is wonderful. You should have seen him with Timmy – they were like old friends at once.'

'Very well. Bobby can stay the night,' said George's mother, and Bobby beamed all over his face.

'If I had a tail I'd wag it hard,' he said, and that made everyone laugh.

Things were soon settled. Mrs Kirrin rang up the police to tell them Bobby was safe. Then she rang up his grandfather and told him the news too. The old man was so relieved that he could hardly thank Mrs Kirrin enough.

'I *wouldn't* have had his dog put to sleep,' he said. 'I just said that to make Bobby more careful with Chummy. Now that the dog's growing so big and strong, he must be properly trained, and must never bite anyone – Bobby's too easy with him. I'll send the dog to a trainer, and when he comes back he'll be quite all right, and Bobby can have him again.'

Bobby didn't think much of this idea when Mrs Kirrin told him.

'I just *won't* let Chummy go to a cruel trainer!' he said, looking round at the others for sympathy.

But even George rounded on him at once. 'There! You care more for your own feelings than for Chummy's well-being! Don't you *want* a dog who's safe even with a small child? Don't you *want* a dog who'll obey you at once, and be a credit to you – like Timmy is to me?'

'All right, all right. Don't bite my head off. Sounds as if *you* ought to go to a trainer too!' said Bobby. 'Going round snapping at people!'

'Mum! I don't want Bobby to stay the night after all!' said George, fiercely.

'Oh *look* at that monkey – he's taken a banana from the dish, and he's peeling it just like a human being!' cried Anne, changing the subject very neatly indeed. 'Aunt Fanny, look – isn't he sweet?'

In the end Bobby was allowed to stay the night, and slept downstairs in the kitchen on a sofa, with Chippy cuddled beside him, and Chummy on his feet. Upstairs George was in bed with Timmy on *her* feet, talking about the excitements of the day with Anne.

'How's your tooth?' asked Anne, suddenly remembering the night before, when George had had such bad toothache, and had wandered about the bedroom, and seen a light on Kirrin Island.

'Tooth? What tooth?' said George, surprised. She had forgotten all about it in the excitement of the afternoon. 'Oh, the one I had out. Doesn't it seem AGES since this morning!'

She put her tongue into the space where the tooth had been. 'I think a new one's growing already,' she said. 'I wish I had teeth like Timmy – snowy white – strong – fierce. I'd like to be able to show all my teeth like Timmy, when I feel really angry!'

Anne laughed. 'Well – you *almost* manage it now,' she said. 'Hey – what's the matter with Timmy? He's pretty restless tonight. Look – he's gone to the door. He wants to go out.'

'All he wants is to go and have a talk to Chummy,' said George. 'All right, Tim. You can go down to the kitchen and sleep with Chummy if you like. I suppose you think he might be lonely. I bet he was scared when he had to hide under that wet, smelly seaweed!'

Timmy pattered down the stairs as soon as the bedroom door was opened. He scraped at the kitchen door and Bobby got up to open it. He was surprised and pleased to see Timmy, who went to lie beside the pleased Alsatian. It wasn't often that Timmy had a doggy visitor and he meant to make the most of it!

George took one more look out of the window before she got into bed – and gave a sudden exclamation.

'Anne – I think there's a light on Kirrin Island again. Anne – come and look!'

'Don't be an idiot,' said Anne, sleepily. 'You don't think we're going to start this adventure all over again, do you? It's FINISHED, George, not just beginning. Come back to bed.'

George jumped into bed. 'It *was* a light,' she said, after a moment or two. 'But only a shooting star!

What a pity! I'd have liked another adventure – wouldn't you, Anne?'

But Anne was fast asleep, dreaming of monkeys, red sandals, seaweed, big dogs and orange peel.

Well – I'm not really surprised at that – are you?

*Discover the World
of the Famous Five . . .*

The Famous Five Through the Years

1942   The first Famous Five novel was published
        – *Five On a Treasure Island*. For many years,
        the books were available in hardback
        editions, which are now highly collectible.

1950   *Five on a Treasure Island* was published in
        America. Since then, the books have been
        translated into many languages and sold all
        around the world.

1952   The hugely successful Famous Five club
        began, as part of Enid Blyton's charitable
        works to help children recovering from
        illness. Thousands of children joined and
        their   fund-raising   eventually   helped

establish a Famous Five ward at Great Ormond Street Hospital in London.

1955   Enid Blyton wrote a stage play about the Famous Five, which was performed at Princes Theatre in London – she helped cast the children in the starring roles, and attended several of the rehearsals. Also in this year, the Famous Five was published in France.

1957   *Five On a Treasure Island* was produced as eight sixteen-minute films by the Children's Film Foundation.

1963   Enid Blyton published the last of the Famous Five novels – *Five Are Together Again* – which was the 21st in the series.

1964   The Children's Film Foundation released *Five Have a Mystery to Solve* as six films.

1967   The Famous Five were published in paperback editions for the first time by Knight.

1975   Philips released the first Famous Five LP record, *Five on a Treasure Island*.

1977   The first *Famous Five Annual* was published, based on *Famous Five on a Hike Together*, told in a mix of illustrated text and a comic strip.

1978-9 Southern Television broadcast hugely popular dramatisations of all but three of the books.

1983   Rainbow released the first dramatised cassette of the Famous Five, *Five Run Away Together*.

1985 *Enid Blyton's Adventure Magazine* was published, with cartoons based on the stories.

1995-7 A brand new TV series saw all the novels adapted by Zenith North.

1996 The Famous Five Musical (based on *Five Go Adventuring Again*) toured around Britain. The first Famous Five CD-ROM, *Five on a Treasure Island*, was released by S.I.R.

1997 To mark Enid Blyton's centenary, the Royal Mail issued a set of stamps, one of which featured the Famous Five.

2008 Disney launched a TV cartoon series featuring the children of the Famous Five. Sometimes, the original characters and stories are referenced, but they bear little resemblance to Enid Blyton's originals.

2012   Hodder Children's Books celebrated the Five's 70th anniversary with special editions featuring covers by Quentin Blake, Helen Oxenbury, Emma Chichester Clark, Chris Riddell and Oliver Jeffers – in association with the charity House of Illustration.

About Enid Blyton

Enid Mary Blyton was born on 11 August, 1897 in a small flat over a shop in Lordship Lane, East Dulwich, London. When she was only a few months old the family moved to Beckenham in Kent, an area where Enid and her brothers, Hanly and Carey, spent their childhood. Growing up, she loved spending time outdoors – and reading and writing.

She began publishing her work in 1917, and by the early 1920s she had a regular column in a magazine for teachers. (Later, she went on to write two magazines of her own.) Her first book was a collection of poems, *Child Whispers* which came out in 1922.

In 1937, Enid decided to try out a serial story in her magazine. She called it *Adventures of the Wishing*

Chair, and it was so popular with readers that she decided to follow it up with another – an adventure story called *The Secret Island*. Soon hundreds of readers were writing in demanding more adventures of Jack, Mike, Peggy and Nora.

Enid and Hugh had two daughters, Gillian and Imogen, but the couple divorced and Enid married again. By now she was in the busiest period of her life. She wrote school stories and circus stories but best of all her readers loved her adventure and mystery novels. Some of the most popular were The Famous Five and The Secret Seven.

During the last few years of her life Enid suffered from poor health. She died on 28 November 1968, but has been warmly remembered ever since. Her bestselling books are still amongst children's favourites today.

The Famous Five's Fans

After publishing so many poems and short stories, Enid Blyton was surprised at how popular her first series book, *The Secret Island*, proved to be. So many children wrote to her to say that they wanted more adventures about characters they could get to know over a series of books.

By far the most popular of the series she created was the Famous Five! Enid's idea was to write just six books. She was always in touch with her readers – she loved meeting them at events, and receiving letters from them – who demanded more. So she wrote another six, but that wasn't enough, either! In total, she wrote twenty-one novels about Julian, Dick, Anne, George and Timothy, the dog – and eight short stories.

FIVE HAVE A PUZZLING TIME

A lot of children asked Enid if the characters were based on real people. Sometimes, after writing a book, she realized that a character who she thought was made up was based on someone she knew. At the end of her autobiography, Enid wrote:

'George . . . was also a real girl. You will remember that she is called Georgina but refuses to be called anything but George, because she so badly wants to be a boy. I think you must have felt she was real, because so often in your letters you say to me, "George *is* real, isn't she?" . . .

'The real George was short-haired, freckled, sturdy, and snub-nosed. She was bold and daring, hot-tempered and loyal. She was sulky, as George is too, but she isn't now. We grow out of those failings – or we should! Do you like George? I do.'

Many years after this was written, Enid admitted that George was based on herself when young.

As you can see from the timeline in this book, the Famous Five had a life beyond the printed page – with games, television series, films and plays. During Enid's lifetime, the books also formed the core of a special club which Enid set up in response to requests from her fans. To announce the club, her publishers, Hodder & Stoughton, printed a special bookmark to be inserted in the brand new title, *Five Have a Wonderful Time*, and also in reprints of other Famous Five novels.

Her publishers sent out membership kits and later prizes. In her letter to the club members, Enid wrote:

'Now the reason for starting the club is this: everywhere I go I meet boys and girls who are already my friends because they are friends of the Famous Five. There are hundreds of thousands of you all over the world. The great pity is that I can't recognize you, and you don't recognize each other, which is why, of course, you have begged so often for a badge. And now at last we have one.

'If all our members wear their badges we shall know each other at once, and I shall be able to recognize you too. I shall come up to you and speak to you, so look out for me! I shall wear my badge too, of course, so you shall always know me.

'Quite a lot of children have suggested a signal of some kind when you see someone else wearing the FF badge – such as raising your hand, spreading your five fingers quickly and dropping your hand again. I think I will leave you to think of your own signal, and as the Club grows we shall see which signal becomes the most popular. It is your Club, and I want you to think out good ideas for it.'

Enid wanted the club to have another purpose, so the membership fees first went to help the Children's Convalescent Home in Beaconsfield. The club also had its own magazine with a news-sheet and a puzzle page.

By 1959, the club had over one hundred thousand members! Enid Blyton's legacy has been looked after by her estate since her death, and the club was still running, in a different form, until 1990.

*Look out for more special editions,
with wonderful new covers by
favourite illustrators . . .*

More classic stories from the world of

Enid Blyton

The Famous Five

The adventures of Julian, Dick, Anne, George and Timmy have been delighting readers for over 70 years. There are twenty-one adventures – full of mystery, suspense, danger and surprise.

Five On Kirrin Island Again
– cover by Shirley Hughes

What is Uncle Quentin up to on Kirrin Island? He won't let anyone visit – not even the Famous Five! But he's not alone on George's island – somebody is watching his every move!

Can Julian, Anne, Dick, George and Timmy the dog find out who and warn Uncle Quentin?

Five Go Off to Camp
– cover by David Tazzyman

Spook trains in the dead of night! And they seem to
vanish into thin air – but where do they go? The
Famous Five are on to it! But the discovery of an
unusual underground tunnel system and a secret
train-service has them puzzled. If they follow the
tracks, will they solve the mystery?

Five Get Into Trouble
– cover by Polly Dunbar

The Famous Five are distraught! Dick has been
kidnapped – mistaken for somebody else! The gang
finally track him down – to a lonely, abandoned
house – but then they too are seized and held
captive. Now that all of them are miles from home,
and from help, how will the intrepid Five get
themselves out of this mess?

Five Fall Into Adventure
– cover by Babette Cole

Julian, Dick and Anne are really worried –
somebody has broken into Kirrin Cottage and
George and her devoted Timmy have disappeared.
Could there be a connection? The Famous Five
think so, but it's going to be tough getting to the
bottom of this mystery when there's only three of
them . . .

Five On a Hike Together
– cover by Tony Ross

The Famous Five are spending the weekend hiking
in the countryside, when Dick is woken by a flashing
light. Is someone trying to send him a coded
message? And when the Five hear of an escaped
convict in the area, they are on red alert. The police
won't help, so the Five have no choice. Yet again,
they'll be solving this mystery by themselves . . .

As well as the 21 full-length novels,
there are 8 Colour Short Stories:

1. Five and a Half-Term Adventure
2. George's Hair is Too Long
3. Good Old Timmy
4. A Lazy Afternoon
5. Well Done, Famous Five
6. Five Have a Puzzling Time
7. Happy Christmas, Five
8. When Timmy Chased the Cat

Illustrated by Jamie Littler, published by
Hodder Children's Books

More classic stories from the world of

Enid Blyton

The Naughtiest Girl

Elizabeth Allen is spoilt and selfish. When she's sent away to boarding school she makes up her mind to be the naughtiest pupil there's ever been! But Elizabeth soon finds out that being bad isn't as simple as it seems. Thre are ten brilliant books about the Naughtiest Girl to enjoy.

More classic stories from the world of

Enid Blyton

The Secret Seven

Join Peter, Janet, Jack, Barbara, Pam, Colin, George
and Scamper as they solve puzzles and mysteries,
foil baddies, and rescue people from danger – all without
help from the grown-ups. Enid Blyton wrote fifteen
stories about the Secret Seven. These editions contain
brilliant illustrations by Tony Ross, plus extra
fun facts and stories to read and share.

Reading Tips

The **National Literacy Trust** is a charity that transforms lives through literacy. We want to get more families reading. Reading is fun and children who read in their own time do better at school and later in life. By partnering with McDonald's, we hope to encourage more families to read together.

Here are some of our top tips for reading with children.

A good way to bring a book to life is to put on different voices for different characters in the story.

Why not stop at certain points in the story to ask your child what *they* think will happen next?

Setting aside some time to read with your child every day is something both of you can look forward to.

A shared love of reading can last a lifetime. You can still read aloud to your child, even when they are confident enough to read by themselves.

If your child is excited by the subject of a story, it will help keep their interest as you read together, so help them choose the books you'll read together.